Move It!

Alan Trussell-Cullen

Contents

Chapter 1	How Things Move	4
Chapter 2	People and Machines	8
Chapter 3	How They Move	10
Chapter 4	Push or Pull?	14
Glossary and Index		16

Chapter 1

HOW THINGS MOVE

Push

Things can be moved by pushing them.

This **bulldozer** is pushing over the tree.

This girl is pushing her friend on the swing.

This man is pushing a rolling pin.

Pull

Things can be moved by pulling them.

The car is pulling the **caravan**.

The dogs are pulling the sled.

The hammer is pulling the nail.

The boat is pulling the ship.

Chapter 2

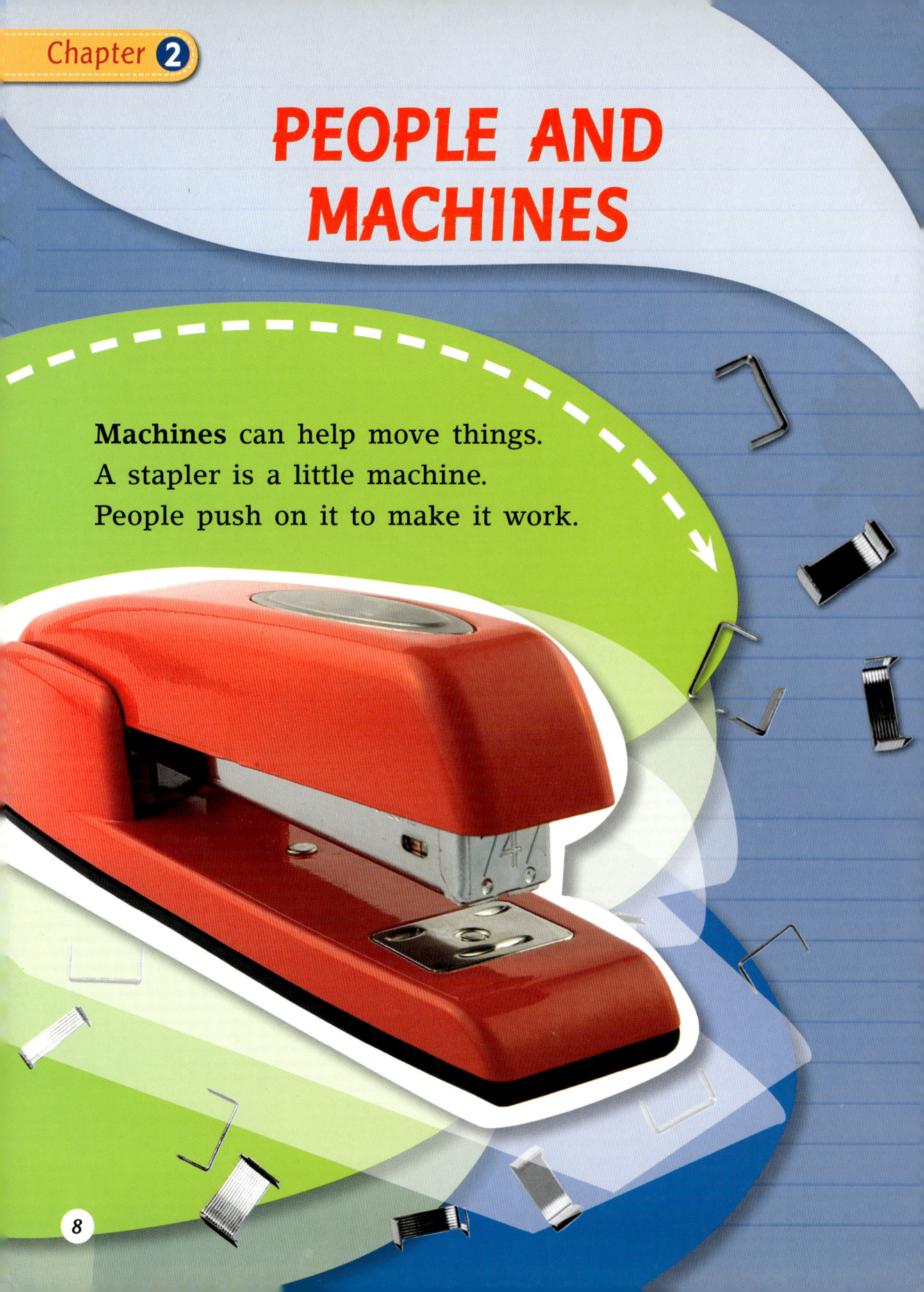

PEOPLE AND MACHINES

Machines can help move things.
A stapler is a little machine.
People push on it to make it work.

A crane is a big machine.
People use cranes to pull things up.

Chapter 3
HOW THEY MOVE

How Skateboards Move

The boy pushes with his foot.
The push makes the skateboard move.

11

How Birds Move

The bird moves its wings.
The wings push on the **air**.
They make the bird move.

How Balloons Move

The boy lets the balloons go. The air inside the balloons pushes on the air outside the balloons. The balloons take off.

Chapter 4

PUSH OR PULL?

Look at these pictures.
Push or pull?

1

2

③

④

Answers: 1. Pull, 2. Push, 3. Push, 4. Pull.

15

Glossary

air   air is a gas all around us. We cannot see it but we breathe it in and out.

bulldozer   a large machine used to push things

caravan   a home on wheels that can be pulled from place to place

machine   a machine is a thing that does work for us

Index

balloons 13
birds 12
bulldozer 4
caravan 6
cars 6
crane 9

dogs 6
machines 8, 9
skateboards 10–11
stapler 8
swing 4